HOW TO BE ON THE MOON

To Steph P

First published 2019 by Walker Books Ltd
87 Vauxhall Walk, London SE11 5HJ

This edition published 2020

2 4 6 8 10 9 7 5 3 1

© 2019 Viviane Schwarz

The right of Viviane Schwarz to be identified as the author/illustrator of this work has been asserted by her in accordance with the Copyright, Designs and Patents Act 1988

This book has been typeset in ITC Stone Informal and Birch

Printed in China

British Library Cataloguing in Publication Data: a catalogue record for this book is available from the British Library

ISBN 978-1-4063-8310-2

www.walker.co.uk

HOW TO BE ON THE MOON

VIVIANE SCHWARZ

WALKER BOOKS
AND SUBSIDIARIES
LONDON · BOSTON · SYDNEY · AUCKLAND

"LET'S GO TO THE MOON!" said Anna.

"But that's out in space," said Crocodile. "Space is dark, and there's nobody there, and the moon is really very far away. It will be almost impossible."

"I like that," said Anna. "Let's go!"

"Hang on," said Crocodile. "We will need special skills to go to the moon."

"What skills?" asked Anna.

"Maths. Without maths, it will go wrong."

"I can do maths," said Anna.

"Can you count backwards?" asked Crocodile.

"Five, four, three, two, one," Anna said. "Zoom!"

"Wait," said Crocodile. "We will also have to be almost impossibly patient to go to the moon. It is a very long journey."

"I can do that," said Anna. "Watch me. Am I patient yet?"

"No," said Crocodile.

"And now?"   —"No."

"And now?"   —"No."

"And now?"   —"No."

"And now?"   —"No."

"And now?"   —"Still not."

"And now?"   —"No."

"And now?"   —"No."

"And now?"   —"No."

"And now?"   —"No."

"Well, YOU are very patient," Anna said. "That'll do for both of us. Let's go!"

"Maybe we should take some travel games along," said Crocodile.

"Now we are ready to go to the moon!" said Anna.

"Are you sure?" Crocodile asked. "We will need to travel at almost impossible speed. Otherwise we will run out of sandwiches on the way."

"You make the sandwiches, I will make the speed," said Anna.

Anna built a rocket.

Crocodile made sandwiches…

"Ten, nine, eight, seven, six, five,
four, three, two, one, ZOOM!"

And they blasted off to the moon.

"Are we there soon?"
Anna asked.

"No," said Crocodile.
"Let's play cards."

The cards wouldn't
stay on the table.
Neither would the
sandwiches.

"Let's play Crocodiles
in Space," said Anna,
and they did. The
rules were: If you
caught all the parts
of a sandwich, you
got to eat the
sandwich. If you
caught anything else,
it didn't taste as nice.

They both won.

"We must be there soon," said Anna.

But the moon was still far away.

"I am very patient," said Anna. "Look."

"It's hard to tell," said Crocodile, "but I believe you."

"Maybe I would be even more patient if I were asleep," said Anna.

"Probably," said Crocodile. "I will wake you up when we get there."

"Now we are
nearly there,"
said Crocodile.

Anna woke up.
"Prepare to land!"

Crocodile
pressed the
landing button.

Anna pulled the
landing lever.

They held on
tight and...

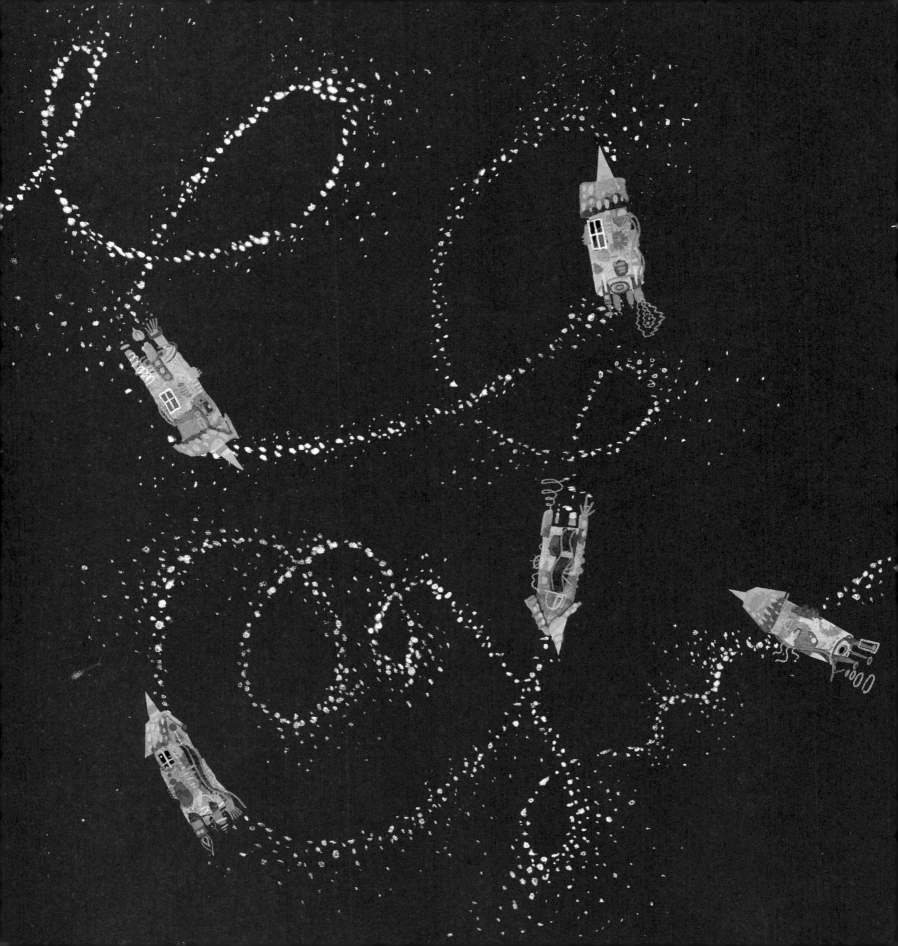

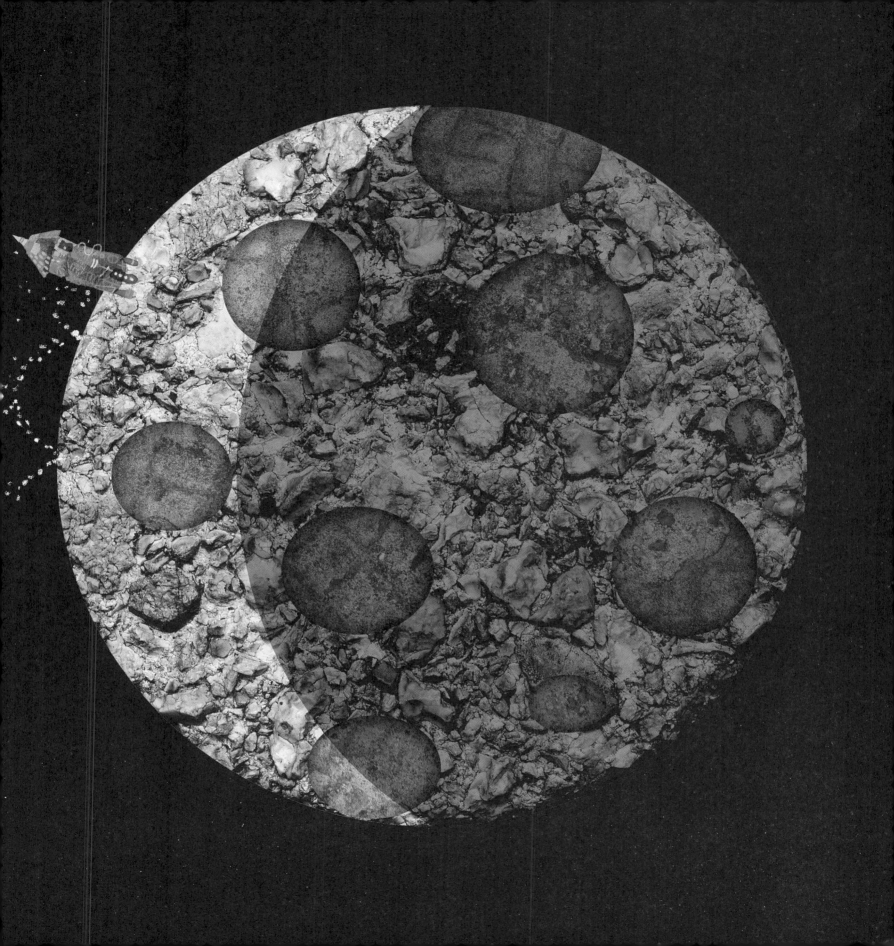

"The moon! We are on the moon!" said Anna.

"Eat another sandwich before putting on your space helmet," said Crocodile. "It's difficult afterwards."

They put on their space suits and went out to explore.

"There really is no one here," said Crocodile.

"You are here," said Anna, "and so am I."

"True," said Crocodile.

"And it's not dark," said Anna.

"The Earth is shining," said Crocodile.

They looked up at the Earth.

"It's almost impossibly beautiful," said Crocodile.

"But so small," said Anna. "How can Earth be so small?"

"It's just very far away," said Crocodile.

"Being far away feels just the same as being very small when you're missing someone," said Anna.

"Do you think it misses us?"

"Of course! We are on the moon!"

"Poor Earth."

"Let's fly back," said Anna.

"Yes, let's," said Crocodile.

So they went back home.

"Earth!" said Crocodile. "We are on Earth!"

"We went to the moon!" said Anna. "It was almost impossible!"

"But we had the skills!"

"And now we are back home! You can stop worrying. Look, the Earth is everywhere! It is huge!"

"I'm not worried. You always stayed the right size," said Crocodile. "That's the main thing."

"You too," said Anna. "We are very good at that. Let's go and check on the rest of the world, just in case."

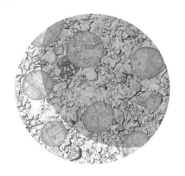

And they did.